The Coldvir-20 Killer

Martin Lundqvist

Published by Martin Lundqvist, 2020.

This is a work of fiction. Similarities to real people, places, or events are entirely coincidental.

THE COLDVIR-20 KILLER

First edition. October 26, 2020.

Copyright © 2020 Martin Lundqvist.

Written by Martin Lundqvist.

The Coldvir-20 Killer

"No Grandma! Why did you die so young?"

The effeminate hipster Nathan Mortimer wiped a tear from his eyes with his facemask, exposing the green-dyed beard below. The few times Nathan had ever reflected over his grandmother's passing, he had always seen it as a Hollywood moment. In his vision, the whole family had gathered at her deathbed to hear her final words. The reality was much bleaker. Nathan's parents were out of state and they had no intention to return to Victoria and indefinite house arrest to see the old beloved lady croak over. As for Nathan he had been too late to the hospital. Spending his last money on soy lattes had been an unwise move as he couldn't afford an Uber ride to the hospital.

A female doctor approached Nathan and spoke:

- So, you must be Emma's grandson? I am sorry about the loss of your grandma, but I can assure you she didn't suffer.

The doctor's nonchalant attitude angered Nathan and he exclaimed:

- Mmphhr, fuckmws, hmmph.

The doctor gave him a confused look and replied:

- Pardon me?

Nathan took off his face diaper and replied:

- I am sorry. I can't speak properly through the facemask when I am upset.

A nurse came rushing towards them with a new facemask, but the doctor waved her away, took off her mask, and gave Nathan a sympathetic smile. The doctor said:

- I understand. It is hard to lose someone. However, she lived longer than most and she died peacefully. Were you close to her?

Nathan reflected over his answer. He had never been close to his grandma because she came from an Eastern European communist country and she had a thick foreign accent. Worst of all, she disliked communism and the self-proclaimed Supreme Leader of the state of Victoria, Ms Danielle Anders. Nathan:

- Not really. But it is hard to lose someone so early. I thought we would have many years to mend our broken relationship.

The doctor gave Nathan a confused look and replied:

- Lose someone so early? Emma was 95 years old and she had cancer, diabetes, and kidney failure. It is a miracle that she lived long enough to die from Coldvir-20.

Nathan:

- I don't believe in miracles. I only trust in Marx ideologies, the science, and gender-neutral bathrooms.

Doctor:

- Oh, you are one of those people. I need to get back to my other patients, but the hospital will be in touch so you can organise the funeral of your dear grandmother.

Having said this, the doctor rushed off, realising the pointlessness in arguing with an unemployed radical left-wing hipster, and because she actually had a job to do.

Nathan gave the doctor a death-stare, and feelings off passive-aggressive progressivism overwhelmed him. Nathan wanted revenge. But how could he make the doctor's life miserable through leveraging the powers of cancel culture? The doctor hadn't been racist, homophobic, or denying climate change. Downplaying the tragedy in grandma Emma's death could cause some uproar on Reddit. However, since the doctor had a job, she wouldn't be lurking in the left wing forums in any case.

When Nathan was reflecting over his revenge, his eyes caught something crucial. It was a list of people that had tested positive for Cold virus 20 in Brunswick, Victoria in the latest month. His grandmother had lived at a nursing home in Brunswick and one of the people on this list could be the careless science-denier that had murdered his grandmother through spreading the terrible virus. Filled with a new purpose in life, Nathan grabbed the list, determined to find his grandma's murderer.

STATE PREMIER DANIELLE Anders, also known as Dictator Danielle, was trying to keep a stern and solemn face, although she was bubbling with joy on the inside, as she gave the daily virus update in front of her loyal reporters from the press. Her loyal Chief Medical Officer, Professor Button, who wasn't a real professor, had tested enough elderly people to find 650 individuals that were infected with Coldvir-20 when they died. 650 was an ideal number. It was enough deaths to justify a CCP-inspired police state led by Danielle. Yet it was fewer Coldvir-20 deaths than some other nations, showing that her lockdowns were working. Danielle:

> - So, sadly 650 people died with Coldvir-20 in August. I have tried my best to keep this number down, but unfortunately, we have a lot of people that don't believe in masks and indefinite house arrest. Because of these selfish people, I will ask the parliament to grant me even more powers to deal with this terrible virus. Any questions?

Danielle felt aggression shaking her to the core when her rival from Sky News, Alana Tones took off her mask and revealed her face. Alana spoke towards the premier:

- I have a question about the death numbers. In August 2019 Victoria had 4000 deaths, of which 650 deaths stated "old age" as the primary reason. This year Victoria had 4000 deaths, but none of them states "old age" on the death certificate. Did "Professor" Button relabel last year's death statistics, changing "old age" to "Coldvir-20"?

Danielle had an epiphany. "Professor" Button was a full-blown idiot and he didn't even know how to lie with credibility. Relabelling all "old age" deaths as Coldvir deaths? Any sensible person would manipulate statistics better than that. Being a seasoned politician and serial liar, Danielle tried changing the topic:

- I don't like how you insinuate that old people's lives don't matter. But tell me this, how many people under 30 died of "old age" last year?

Alana gave Danielle a sceptical look and replied:

- None, of course, what a ridiculous question.

Danielle looked at her presentation and was ready to swing the axe on Alana when she made a terrible realisation. No-one under the age of 30 had died with Coldvir-20 in August. Ouch. Danielle wasn't going to concede so she said:

- Thus, I can guarantee you that anyone below 30 who dies from Coldvir-20 wouldn't have died from old age otherwise. A few young people will be dying soon, proving that this virus is very lethal to everyone. This marks the end of this press conference. I would appreciate it if Sky News didn't undermine my hard work to keep Victorians safe. Dismissed.

Having said this, Danielle put on her facemask. Unfortunately, the strap to her facemask got stuck in her microphone, causing both the mic and Danielle to fall to the floor. Ouch!

NATHAN MORTIMER WAS watching the press conference on his iPad in the safety of his home, far away from all the selfish plague carriers outside. His Centrelink payment had landed in his account and this made him feel a bit better about himself. In an hour, he would mask up and head to a local coffee shop for a takeaway soy latte. The local coffee shop had a coffee happy hour between 3 and 4pm. Besides, fewer virus spreaders were waiting for coffee at that time of the day.

Danielle's words on the press conference had given Nathan a double purpose in life. He could avenge his grandma through murdering enough young people with Coldvir-20 to prove that the virus was dangerous to everyone. If he played his cards right, Victoria could be in lockdown for another year, paving the path for the future communist utopia with Danielle Anders as the Supreme Leader.

Nathan had a brief moment of hesitation. Was it morally correct to go on a murderous spree and terrorise 6 million people because his 95-year-old estranged grandma had died? Wouldn't it be easier to take up contact with his other grandma?

Nathan took up his phone and sent a text message to his grandma Loretta Mortimer: "Hi Grandma. I have terrible news. Grandma Emma died this morning from Coldvir-20. I just wanted to find out whether you are okay."

A few minutes later, Nathan's phone pinged with a voice message: "I thought she died years ago. Don't you worry about me, you pink-haired poof. You're still not in my will. Fuck off. / Loretta"

Ouch.

Realising that he wouldn't inherit any money to keep funding his parasitic lifestyle, Nathan needed to support a communist takeover for his own sake, blissfully unaware that true communists don't appreciate pink-haired parasites either. Nathan added "Contract Coldvir-20 and infect grandma Loretta to punish her for her homophobia" on his to-do list. After that, he left for the coffee shop to feed his caffeine addiction. Once he was caffeinated, he would plan his first murder.

"WE NEED SOME YOUNG people to die from Coldvir-20!" Danielle exclaimed in a private meeting with her Chief Medical Officer "Professor" Button.

Professor Button gave her a confused look and replied:

- Why? How? Do you think a lot of young people die from catching a cold?

Danielle:

- Because someone thought it was a good idea to relabel the statistics of last year's "deaths from old age" to this year's "deaths from Coldvir-20".

Professor Button:

- Oh really. Who would do something that stupid?

Danielle:

- You did, Professor Button.

Professor Button:

- I can't recall doing that?

Danielle:

- You can't recall botching up hotel quarantine either. The Coldvir-20 infected Escort Emily in room 202 at the Grand Chancellor has made $5,000 during quarantine from fucking the guards and police officers that were meant to keep her locked up.

Professor Button:

- To be fair, you have told people to work from home. Emily was following your directive or so, I have been told.

Danielle:

- Gasp! Don't say you slept with her too?!

Professor Button:

- In my defence, she offers very competitive rates, and my dating life has been a bit poor because of the lockdowns.

Danielle:

- So, the cold that you had last month, was it Cold Virus 20?

Professor Button:

- Well, I never got tested so we'll never know.

Danielle:

- You bloody idiot. Do you realise the implications if I get infected from this cold?

Professor Button:

- You'll get a runny nose and you will feel under the weather for a few days?

Danielle:

- I'll look like an idiot. How can I protect the population from this virus by introducing a Chinese Communist Party-style dictatorship if I can't protect myself? I am giving you one chance to redeem yourself "Professor" Button. You need to find some young people that died with Coldvir-20, otherwise, I'll fire you and I'll blame you for the hotel quarantine debacle.

Professor Button:

- Understood, State Premier Anders. I will double my efforts.

Having said this, Professor Button put on his facemask and fled the furious Danielle in terror.

NATHAN MORTIMER WAS outside the house of his first intended victim, Jeffrey Wang. Jeffrey was a 28-year-old lawyer who was Coldvir-20 positive and had visited the same coffee shop as Nathan's grandmother Emma. Could it be Jeffrey who had infected Emma? It was hard to tell, but he fitted the criteria; young and believing that he was safe from the terrible virus. Nathan would prove him otherwise and Jeffrey's positive Coldvir test would be the cause of his death.

Nathan corrected the scrubs that he had stolen from the hospital. For a moment he felt like an important government employee on a mission. Then he recalled that he had never held a job and that his HECS debt was in the six figures due to his Master's degree in gender studies.

Nathan knocked on Jeffrey's door, and a while later, Jeffrey opened it, while wearing a dirty T-shirt with some ramen noodles on it. Nathan cleared his throat and spoke:

- Humph Im Nathanmrrtimetrer.

Jeffrey gave Nathan a curious look and Nathan felt the embarrassment tormenting his mind. Bloody facemask, why did it make it so hard to speak? But then he remembered that one of his goals was to contract Coldvir-20 and give it to his homophobic grandmother, so he took off the facemask and spoke.

- Hi. I am Nathan Mortimer from the Victorian Health Department. I am here to follow up on your Cold Virus 20 diagnosis.

Jeffrey:

- I thought I was meant to self-isolate. Why is a member of the health department standing outside my door without a muzzle?

Nathan:

- Because I am bringing a new experimental wonder drug, courtesy of our friends in the Chinese Communist Party. I had it, and I was immediately cured of Coldvir-20.

Jeffrey:

- But I don't want to get cured. I have a cushy and well-paid government job where I can 'work from home' as long as I don't test negative for Coldvir. Having a slight cold is better than working.

Nathan:

- As a government employee, you must take new experimental drugs to help Premier Danielle Anders eradicate Coldvir.

Jeffrey:

- Very well. Hit me up!

Hearing this, Nathan pulled out the syringe with poison that he had stolen from the hospital. He was about to inject Jeffrey with it when Jeffrey interrupted him.

- Hey? Why does it say 'Coldvir-20 treatment for elderly' if this is a new experimental drug for young people?

Nathan:

- Oh, it's just a typo. Google Translate mixed up the translation from Chinese when we printed the labels. It's meant to say 'Coldvir-20 treatment, not for the elderly'.

Jeffrey:

- That makes sense. Google Translate does that from time to time.

Nathan smiled, nodded, and injected Jeffrey. As Jeffrey collapsed to the floor, Nathan felt a great sense of achievement. He had carried out his first murder and he was one step closer to avenging his grandmother and facilitating a CCP takeover in Victoria.

"CHAIRWOMAN DANIELLE. I have some great news."

Danielle Anders looked up from her desk at 'Professor' Button who had entered her office, without a facemask. She gave him a stern look and replied:

- How dare you enter my office without a facemask? You should be self-isolating after your taxpayer-funded encounter with Emily the Escort.

Professor Button:

- Yes, but I have such great news to share with you. We finally found a young person who died with Coldvir-20.

Danielle:

- This doesn't happen to be Jeffrey Wang who was murdered by a fake nurse administering government-sanctioned opium overdoses?

Professor Button:

- How did you know?

Danielle:

- The police commissioner told me. They found a syringe with 'Coldvir-20 treatment for elderly' next to Jeffrey's body, without his fingerprints on it. Furthermore, our spy drones filmed a fake nurse giving Jeffrey the poison.

Professor Button:

- That is great news. A deluded serial killer will bring up the death rates among the young and we can justify another six months of lockdown.

Danielle:

- But what about Police Commissioner Smitton?

Professor Button:

- Tell him to not investigate Jeffrey's murder. He should focus police resources on arresting people not wearing masks or people whining online about your rule.

Danielle:

- This is a genius plan, Button. This is why I gave an illiterate sycophant an honorary professor title. Let's have some champagne and celebrate our first young person dying from Coldvir-20.

Professor Button:

- With many more to come? Muahaha

Danielle:

- Yes. Muahaha

After saying this, Danielle corked up the champagne and the two of them spent the next hour drinking and laughing evil laughter.

"WE CANNOT LET YOU INTO Grand Chancellor Hotel Quarantine unless you provide a valid medical ID. There is a rumour about a fake nurse murdering Coldvir patients." An uninterested police officer told Nathan.

Nathan turned around a walked off. Murdering Emily the escort was crucial to his plans of avenging his grandma and proving that Coldvir was dangerous to young people. She was, after all, the main source of the Coldvir outbreak in the suburb of Brunswick.

Nathan had an epiphany. While he could not gain access to the hotel as a fake nurse, there was no harm in trying to blend in as a fake security guard. Having come to this conclusion, Nathan went to the dollar store and bought a cheap black T-shirt with 'security' printed on the front and back. He also bought a cheap phone with a sim-card so he could have a fake WhatsApp conversation where he hired himself as a security guard at the Grand Chancellor.

WITH HIS NEW T-SHIRT and fake credentials, Nathan approached the same police officer as before. Nathan:

- Hi. I am here to work as a security guard on level 2. Here is the text message from the guy who hired me.

The police officer looked at the text, gave Nathan a sceptical look, and replied:

- Didn't you try to gain access posing as a fake nurse just an hour ago?

Nathan:

- Absolutely not, it must have been someone else.

Police Officer:

- I see. You bloody lefty hipsters all look the same, don't you? Come on in.

Nathan thought of ranting about the police officer's remark, but he didn't want to draw attention to himself when he was there to commit a murder so he kept calm and carried on.

As Nathan reached level 2 of the Grand Chancellor the Middle Eastern security guard Abdullah approached him:

- Hey, brah. Why are you here? This is a restricted area, brah.

Nathan:

- I am here to work as a security guard. Mahmoud sent me this text.

Abdullah had a quick look at Nathan's phone, gave him a nod and replied:

- Oh, I thought you were one of Emily's clients. I guess I'll have a smoke break then.

Having said this, the guard took the lift down to the lobby and Nathan was free to approach Emily's room.

Nathan knocked on Emily's door and she opened it. The trashy Emily spoke:

- Are you working here or have you come for the Coldvir-20 special? It's $99 for an hour.

Nathan reminded himself that he was against the purchase of sexual favours, and besides, he was broke, so he replied:

- I am working here.

Emily:

- Okay, I'll give you a 15-minute freebie. Make it quick. My best customer, Professor Button, will be here in an hour.

As he watched Emily get undressed, Nathan had a moral dilemma. As a gender studies student, it was reprehensible that he visited a woman of the night. On the other hand, he was a virgin about to become a serial killer so he had already thrown the morals out the window. After doing the deed with Emily, Nathan smothered her with a pillow and left the Grand Chancellor Hotel, after stealing her money.

DANIELLE ANDERS WAS drinking red wine and reading the Communist Manifesto in her tax-funded mansion when Professor Button stormed in. As per usual, he was not wearing a facemask. "The shit I have to put up with," Danielle mumbled to herself as Button rushed up to her and exclaimed:

- Emily the Escort is dead. Someone raped and murdered her.

Danielle nodded with an afterthought and replied:

- Emily was the source of the Brunswick Coldvir outbreak, wasn't she? Was she still Coldvir positive?

Professor Button:

- Yes, if we crank up the number of cycles on the PCR test. Emily was positive after cycle 70 on her last test.

Danielle:

- Well, that's great news. Two people under 30 dying with Coldvir in a single day. We are making progress.

Professor Button:

- But she was murdered and we know who her killer is. Our facial recognition software identified a certain Nathan Mortimer as both the fake nurse who killed Jeffrey and the fake security guard who killed Emily.

Danielle:

- Well, we have to classify this investigation. We cannot arrest this Nathan until I have convinced the parliament to give me another six months of emergency powers. After that, we can write a retraction note where we admit that a serial killer caused our Coldvir deaths.

Professor Button:

- Understood. But we must punish Nathan for killing Emily. She was so young, lively, and good in bed. Speaking of which, do you mind if I stay here and share that bottle of red wine with you?

Danielle:

- I do mind. Get the hell out of my mansion, Professor Button.

Being reprimanded by his fearsome boss, Professor Button fled the mansion in terror.

NATHAN MORTIMER EXPERIENCED orgasmic feelings of bliss and joy, stroking a copy of Mao's Little Red Book while watching the latest Danielle Anders press conference. With two deaths in the last 24 hours, Danielle drove the point that lockdowns were crucial to saving humanity from extinction. In a few days, the lockdowns would be extended for another six months and this would crush the capitalists and introducing the socialist paradise.

Nathan, however, wasn't satisfied with only two Coldvir deaths. He had higher goals. On the list of Coldvir infected in Brunswick, there were three people that Nathan went to high school with. They were impoverished drug addicts who were living in a locked-down social housing tower close to his late grandmas nursing home. Emma had used to complain about marijuana smoke from the social housing complex. Chances were that the virus particles had accompanied the smoke and infected his grandma.

Nathan shaved off his green beard and he put on a hoodie with an aboriginal hip hop brand. If he were to pass through the police checkpoint guarding the social housing complex, he needed to blend in. He used a label maker to print new labels for the poison, overwriting 'Coldvir-20 treatment for elderly' with a label saying 'Good Smack, brah'

Having made his plan, Nathan started walking towards the social housing complex. As he reached the social housing police checkpoint, one of the police officers approached him and spoke:

- Hey, aren't you Nathan Mortimer? Why did you shave off your beard?

Nathan froze. How could the police officer recognise him through his facemask? Did this mean that they knew about his other murders? Nathan decided to try a bluff:

- I am doing some counselling with the prisoners, uhm residents, of this house. You know, keeping them mentally healthy to stop suicides.

Police officer:

- Caseworkers are not visiting clients at 2 AM.

Nathan:

- Uhm, I am dealing drugs so the prisoners, uhm residents don't die from heroin withdrawal. It's a matter of life and death.

Hearing this the police officer drew his gun and exclaimed:

- Freeze! Hands up slimeball. Get down on the ground.

Nathan sighed. If he got caught, the communist revolution might fail, which would be such a terrible outcome for the people of the glorious state of Victoria.

An intervention occurred that helped Nathan get back in control. Someone called the policeman over the radio and when his conversation had finished, he approached Nathan:

- Sorry about the inconvenience, Mr Mortimer. Police Commissioner Smitton just issued you with a night pass to the building.

Nathan smiled and replied:

- Thanks, Officer. You are doing the state of Victoria a great favour.

Having said this, Nathan took the lift to level 12 of the social housing complex where his next victims, the Sharika Brothers, resided.

As Nathan knocked on the door, Brendan Sharika opened the door, and the pungent smell of hashish and sweat reached Nathan's nostrils. Brendan stared at him in amazement and exclaimed:

- Nathan Mortimer, fucking oath. What are you doing here, pooftah?

Nathan:

- Danielle Anders sent me to compensate you for locking you up as prisoners in your own homes. I have brought you syringes of good hospital grade smack.

Brendan:

- Bloody legend, mate. Come in and say hello to the boys.

Nathan entered the room, and to his great relief, there were two others in the apartment. No-one questioned why Nathan brought them free drugs, and a while later the Sharika Brothers lay dead on the apartment floor. "Triple kill," Nathan mumbled to himself and left the complex.

"MWAH"

Professor Button experienced a mixture of shock and joy when Premier Danielle Anders kissed him during the morning briefing. He reciprocated and kissed her huge ear before he whispered:

- We can do more than kissing, Premier Danielle.

Danielle shrugged it off, took a step back, and replied:

- No, don't worry about that. I was just so happy that three more young people died of Coldvir-20 last night. A hattrick!

Professor Button:

- How did this happen?

Danielle:

- Nathan Mortimer. He is such a genius. He snuck into the locked-down social housing complex in Brunswick and killed three infected junkies with stolen Coldvir-20 treatment syringes for elderly. If he wasn't a deranged murderous lunatic, I would be in love.

Professor Button:

- So, what happens now?

Danielle:

- The vote in parliament regarding my emergency powers is tomorrow. After I have won six more months of dictatorship, I will instruct Police Commissioner Smitton to arrest Nathan Mortimer.

Professor Button:

- Seems like you got it all figured out. Should I tell my men to keep testing dying elderly people for Coldvir-20?

Danielle:

- Of course. Did you ever stop?

Professor Button:

- Yes, I thought the goal was to kill young people now?

Danielle:

- Argh. You are hopeless. I command you to travel to Brunswick and administer the treatment at the local nursing home at once. I need those deaths for my press conference. Dismissed.

NATHAN MORTIMER WOKE up with a sore throat and this filled him with joy. After murdering Coldvir infected patients, he had finally contracted the elusive virus himself. It was time to visit and kill his homophobic grandmother Loretta.

Nathan drove to Loretta's mansion in Toorak. It was a blemish on his reputation as a left-wing progressive, that his grandmother was wealthy and homophobic.

Nathan knocked on Loretta's door and she came to answer it. Loretta studied Nathan, smiled, and spoke:

- So, you finally shaved off that hideous green beard? Now you need to get a haircut and some proper clothes and then you can get a real job.

Nathan:

- That's never going to happen, grandma. The fights against global warming and for gender-neutral bathrooms are way too important for me to work for the capitalists who are exploiting the workers.

Loretta:

- Very well. You are not receiving any inheritance then. So why did you come?

Nathan smelled a flower to trigger his pollen allergy and then he sneezed his grandma in the face. Achu!
Nathan:

- I came to share the news. I am Coldvir-20 infected and soon you will be too. Your money and capitalism can't save you from this.

Loretta:

- Bloody phony communist. The only thing you shared in your life is your cold viruses. Get the fuck out of here!

Nathan smirked and left Loretta's mansion. He had punished her for her homophobic capitalist ideals. He would become a hero on his Reddit forum. Unfortunately for Nathan, his cold virus-20 infection did contribute to his death. He sneezed while driving past a red light, and a truck hit his car. Rest in Peace, Nathan.

DANIELLE ANDERS TOOK a deep breath of relief when she found out about Nathan's death before she was giving her daily press conference. Since Nathan was dead, there was no police case anymore, and she could keep up the charade that Coldvir-20 had killed five young people in four days. As she entered the press conference, her rival, the political reporter Alana Tones asked her:

- Premier Anders. Do you have any comment on Police Commissioner Smitton's statement that your recent Coldvir-20 deaths were people murdered by the deranged lunatic Nathan Mortimer?

Danielle stared at Commissioner Smitton in disbelief. Why had he exposed the truth the day before her dictatorial powers came into effect? Smitton smiled at her, and Danielle realised her mistake, hiring incompetent sycophants could occasionally backfire.

'Time to apply emergency plan 2B.' Danielle thought and she simulated a coughing fit. Cough! Cough! Cough!

Danielle:

- Oh no, I have caught Coldvir-20 and I consider everyone in this room to be close contacts. You'll all need to visit hotel quarantine.

Having said this, Danielle left the room while her health inspector goons stormed in with hazmat suits and captured everyone. Using the confusion to her advantage, Danielle drove off to the airport where a private jet took her to China.

A FEW DAYS LATER, THE former Premier Danielle Anders met with Chairman Jing Xi of the Chinese Communist Party. Danielle bowed in front of Jing Xi and spoke:

- Thank you for granting me asylum in China, Chairman Xi.
- I was so close to achieving our goals for Australia.

Jing Xi:

- That's alright, Danielle. You achieved more than we ever believed you would. Victoria and Australia will be ours.

Danielle:

- I am glad to hear that, Chairman. Do you have any important jobs for me to do here?

Jing Xi:

- Yes. You'll become the kidney of my concubine Sara, and the liver of her mother Michelle. An honourable task.

Danielle:

- But wait, won't this kill me?

Jing Xi:

- Yes. Muahaha.

Danielle:

- No! Please have mercy.

Jing didn't reply. Instead, his goons stormed in and grabbed Danielle, so she could keep serving the CCP through providing the organs to Jing Xi's concubines.

THE END.

Don't miss out!

Visit the website below and you can sign up to receive emails whenever Martin Lundqvist publishes a new book. There's no charge and no obligation.

https://books2read.com/r/B-A-QIOG-AMRJB

BOOKS 2 READ

Connecting independent readers to independent writers.

Also by Martin Lundqvist

Divine Space Gods
Divine Space Gods: Abraham's Follies
Divine Space Gods II: Revolution for Dummies
Divine Space Gods III: Rangda's Shenanigans

Sabina räddar framtiden
Sabinas jakt på den heliga graalen

Sabina Saves the Future
Sabina's Pursuit of The Holy Grail
Sabina's Quest to Open the Portal in the Sun Pyramid
Sabina's Expedition to Stop the Apocalypse

The Banker Trilogy
The Banker and The Dragon
The Banker and the Eagle: The End of Democracy

The Divine Zetan Trilogy
The Divine Dissimulation

The Divine Sedition
The Divine Finalisation

Standalone
Matt's Amazing Week
James Locker The Duality of Fate
The Portal in the Pyramid
Money Laundering in the Laundromat
Pyramidportalen
Matts Fantastiska Vecka
Divine Space Gods Trilogy
Sabina Saves the Future: Complete Trilogy
Diez Historias Aleatorias y Muy Cortas
Ten Random and Very Short Stories
10 zufällige Kurzgeschichten Volumen 1
Dieci Storie Casuali e Molto Brevi
Dix Histoires Aléatoires et Très Courtes
Cinco Historias Aleatorias y Muy Cortas
Five Random and Very Short Stories
The Fall of Martin Orchard
Masa Depan Putri Sabina
La Caída de Martin Orchard
El Banquero y el Dragón
A Sedição Divina
Dieci storie casuali e molto brevi. Vol 2
Δέκα Τυχαίες και πολύ Σύντομες Ιστορίες Volume 2
The Coldvir-20 Killer
10 zufällige Kurzgeschichten Volumen 2

Watch for more at martinlundqvist.com.